This Walker book belongs to:

____

____

to my teachers
past, present, and future

First published in Great Britain 2019
by Walker Books Ltd, 87 Vauxhall Walk,
London SE11 5HJ

10 9 8 7 6 5 4 3

First published in the United States 2019
by Hyperion Books for Children, an imprint of Disney
Book Group. British publication rights arranged with
Wernick & Pratt Agency, LLC.

This book is hand-lettered
and typeset in Alleycat ICG

Printed in China

A catalogue record for this
book is available from the
British Library

ISBN 978-1-4063-8901-2

www.walker.co.uk

The Pigeon
HAS to Go
School!
es by mo willems
WALKER BOOKS
AND SUBSIDIARIES
LONDON • BOSTON • SYDNEY • AUCKLAND

Too late.

Rats...

Why do *I* have
to go to school?

I already know EVERYTHING!

Go on - ask me
a question.

Well, I know *almost* everything.

Does "school" start in the morning?

Because you *know* what I'm like in the morning!

It is NOT pretty.

I wish
I was
a little
chick
again.

A little-itty-bitty-
not-going-to-school-
baby-waybie pigeon!

What if I don't like school?

What if I REALLY don't like it!?

What if I really, REALLY don't like it!?
WHAT IF-

What if the teacher doesn't like pigeons?

And the STUFF!
What about all
the stuff!?

There is SOOOOOOOOOOO much stuff to learn!

WHAT IF I LEARN TOO MUCH!?!

My head might pop off.

I'm …

scared.

WHAT WILL
AT

HAPPEN

SCHOOL!?

What if there is MATHS?
Or numbers?

Why does the alphabet have so many LETTERS?!
A
B
C
D
M
N
P
WHAT ABOUT LUNCH!?!

READING can be hard with one big eye!

What will
the other
birds THINK
of me?

Will FINGER PAINT
stick to
my feathers?

What's up with
those heavy
BACKPACKS?
I'm a
fragile
bird.

The unknown
stresses me out,
dude.

THERE SHOULD BE A PLACE TO PRACTISE THOSE THINGS!!!

With EXPERTS to help you.

And books.

And classrooms.

And other birds to work and play with.

Maybe a playground.

Oh!
That *is* school.

Well, HOW am I supposed to get there, anyway!?!

Whazza-
Whazza-
WHAAA!?!

Step aside!

Coming through!

The Pigeon HAS to go to school!

Look out for:

978-1-8442-8513-6

978-1-8442-8545-7

978-1-4063-0812-9

978-1-4063-1550-9

978-1-4063-4009-9

978-1-4063-5778-3

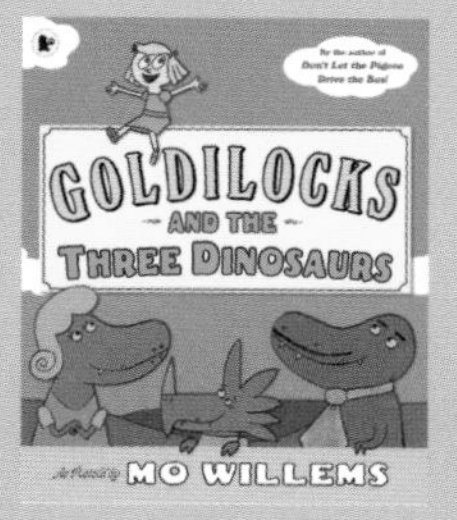

978-1-4063-5532-1

978-1-4063-1215-7

978-1-4063-7963-1

978-1-4063-7369-1

978-1-4063-5558-1

978-1-4063-7621-0

978-1-4063-8358-4

978-1-8442-8059-9

978-1-4063-1382-6

978-1-4063-3649-8